Two powerful hands with claws seized Clint . . .

Hurled into the next room, the Gunsmith crashed into the kitchen table and tumbled to the floor.

Clint had lost the grip on the Springfield. He rose up behind the table and reached for the Colt on his hip. His fingers clutched air . . . the revolver had fallen out of its holster.

He heard the terrible half-wolf, half-human cry of the *chindi* as the outline of a nightmare figure appeared at the doorway.

The Gunsmith saw the shaggy, fur-covered shape with the snarling wolf snout and pointed ears approach him.

The *chindi* had come back for the kill. . . .

**Don't miss any of the lusty, hard-riding action in the
Charter Western series, THE GUNSMITH**

1. MACKLIN'S WOMEN
2. THE CHINESE GUNMEN
3. THE WOMAN HUNT
4. THE GUNS OF ABILENE
5. THREE GUNS FOR GLORY
6. LEADTOWN
7. THE LONGHORN WAR
8. QUANAH'S REVENGE
9. HEAVYWEIGHT GUN
10. NEW ORLEANS FIRE
11. ONE-HANDED GUN
12. THE CANADIAN PAYROLL
13. DRAW TO AN INSIDE DEATH
14. DEAD MAN'S HAND
15. BANDIT GOLD
16. BUCKSKINS AND SIX-GUNS
17. SILVER WAR
18. HIGH NOON AT LANCASTER
19. BANDIDO BLOOD
20. THE DODGE CITY GANG
21. SASQUATCH HUNT
22. BULLETS AND BALLOTS

23. THE RIVERBOAT GANG
24. KILLER GRIZZLY
25. NORTH OF THE BORDER
26. EAGLE'S GAP
27. CHINATOWN HELL
28. THE PANHANDLE SEARCH
29. WILDCAT ROUNDUP
30. THE PONDEROSA WAR
31. TROUBLE RIDES A FAST HORSE
32. DYNAMITE JUSTICE
33. THE POSSE
34. NIGHT OF THE GILA
35. THE BOUNTY WOMEN
36. BLACK PEARL SALOON
37. GUNDOWN IN PARADISE
38. KING OF THE BORDER
39. THE EL PASO SALT WAR
40. THE TEN PINES KILLER
41. HELL WITH A PISTOL
42. THE WYOMING CATTLE KILL
43. THE GOLDEN HORSEMAN
44. THE SCARLET GUN

And coming next month:
THE GUNSMITH #46: WILD BILL'S GHOST